A Crabtree Branches Book

Let's Go Fish

SPEARFISHING

By Kerri Mazzarella

CRABTREE
Publishing Company
www.crabtreebooks.com

School-to-Home Support for Caregivers and Teachers

This high-interest book is designed to motivate striving students with engaging topics while building fluency, vocabulary, and an interest in reading. Here are a few questions and activities to help the reader build upon his or her comprehension skills.

Before Reading:

- *What do I think this book is about?*
- *What do I know about this topic?*
- *What do I want to learn about this topic?*
- *Why am I reading this book?*

During Reading:

- *I wonder why...*
- *I'm curious to know...*
- *How is this like something I already know?*
- *What have I learned so far?*

After Reading:

- *What was the author trying to teach me?*
- *What are some details?*
- *How did the photographs and captions help me understand more?*
- *Read the book again and look for the vocabulary words.*
- *What questions do I still have?*

Extension Activities:

- *What was your favorite part of the book? Write a paragraph on it.*
- *Draw a picture of your favorite thing you learned from the book.*

TABLE OF CONTENTS

WHERE TO FISH

Spearfishing is a type of fishing that requires a spear instead of a fishing rod. It takes place in salt water.

It is unlike any other type of fishing. You will be submerged in water while spearfishing. Spearfishing is a fun activity for older kids and adults.

Coral reefs provide a **haven** for fish. Shallow reefs are great places to try spearfishing.

Some people swim out from a boat to spearfish. Others begin right off a beach.

FUN FACTS

The Florida Keys is home to some of the best spearfishing in the U.S.

TYPES OF FISH

The ocean is home to many **species** of fish. Some fish are endangered or protected. Your location will determine the species of fish you are targeting.

grouper

You should only aim and shoot at the fish you plan to keep. Any fish you shoot will likely be injured and not survive.

Some saltwater fish include yellowtail, **hogfish**, grouper, snapper, and halibut. These are all great fish to target while spearfishing. These are also some of the tastiest fish to eat!

hogfish

FUN FACTS

The record hogfish weighing 21.7 pounds (9.8 kg) was speared off the Gulf Coast of Florida.

yellowtail tuna

Pelagic fish, such as tuna and swordfish, are much more difficult to spear. Leave those to the more experienced spearfisher.

SAFETY AND RULES

It is important to have a dive flag to alert other boaters there are divers in the water. Boat motors are the biggest threat to divers in the water.

Spearfishing is more dangerous than other types of fishing. In order to stay safe there are some precautions you need to take.

Never spearfish alone, use the buddy system. It is important to be a strong swimmer and know how to use a mask and **snorkel**.

Be aware of your surroundings. Sharks are attracted to blood. When you shoot a fish be on the lookout and have a plan in case you encounter a shark. Do not panic.

It is important to purchase a spearfishing license. Be aware of restricted areas. You will need to know the size limits and which fish you are permitted to spear before entering the water.

EQUIPMENT AND GEAR

spear gun

A basic spear gun costs about $175, a pole spear costs around $80, and a Hawaiian sling is about $60.

Spearfishing requires very specific gear that is not used in other types of fishing. You will need a spear. There are different options to choose from depending on your experience.

You can use a hand operated kind such as a **pole spear** or Hawaiian sling. Or you can use a gun style.

Hawaiian sling

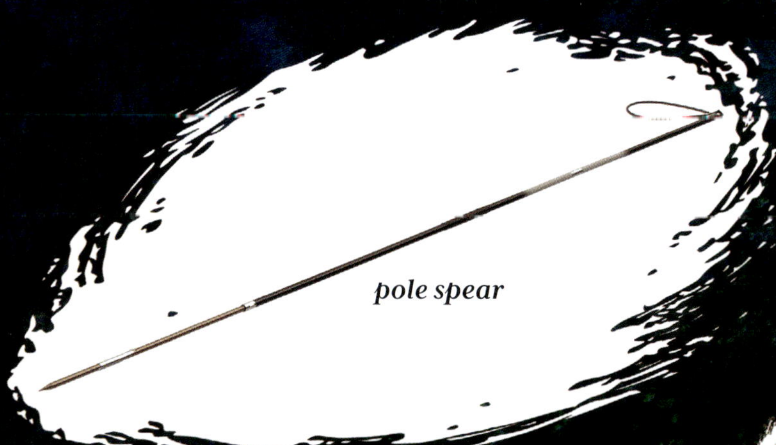

pole spear

Other gear you will need includes a mask, snorkel, **fins,** and gloves. A mask is used to see fish under the water and a snorkel will allow you to breathe while looking for fish. Fins help you swim faster, and gloves will protect your hands while taking fish off your spear.

A mask, snorkel, and fins combo costs $50, and gloves are about $10.

Some spearfishers use a **weight belt**. It helps keep them from floating on the top of the water. It is good to have a dive knife in case you need to cut your spear line. It can also be used as protection from predators.

weight belt

HOW TO SPEARFISH

Spearfishing can be a very fun adventure. Unlike other types of fishing, it requires a great deal of energy because you will be swimming around looking for your fish.

It is best to be prepared. You can watch videos on how to spearfish. There are also many classes available for spearfishing.

For beginners it is best to start off in shallow water and be accompanied by someone who has experience.

FREE DIVING AND SCUBA

Free diving and **scuba** are two ways of spearfishing. The equipment used is much different for each.

Free diving involves holding your breath while you dive down to shoot your fish. It requires some practice and the ability to hold your breath for at least 45 seconds.

Some experienced free divers can easily hold their breath for up to 5 minutes.

Spearfishing with scuba gear allows you to be underwater for long periods of time without coming to the surface for air. This gives you more time to hunt for fish.

You will need to be certified before attempting to scuba dive. The cost to do this is around $250.

Spearfishing is a great way to explore the ocean. With proper gear and the right knowledge, you could be spearfishing in no time. Let the underwater adventure begin!

GLOSSARY

fins (finz): A covering for the foot that has a flat flexible portion made of rubber or plastic to help swim faster

haven (HEY-vuhn): A place of safety

hogfish (HAWG-fish): A species of fish native to the western Atlantic Ocean and found along coral reefs

pelagic (puh-LAJ-ik): Relating to or living in the open ocean

pole spear (POHL speer): An instrument with a long point used in spearing fish

scuba (SKOO-buh): Equipment used for breathing while underwater

snorkel (SNAWR-kuhl): A tube used by swimmers for breathing under water

spearfishing (SPEER-fish-ing): A type of fishing that is done by piercing a fish with a spear

species (SPEE-sheez): A category of things that ranks below a genus

weight belt (WEYT belt): A belt to which weights are attached, designed to help divers stay submerged

INDEX

WEBSITES TO VISIT

https://fishingbooker.com/blog/spearfishing-for-beginners-the-complete-guide/

www.spearfishingtoday.com/spearfishing-beginners/

www.academickids.com/encyclopedia/index.php/speargun

ABOUT THE AUTHOR

Kerri Mazzarella was raised on the east coast of southern Florida. She enjoys all types of fishing. Her family spends weekends on their boat catching fish in the ocean. All four of her teen children are experienced with spearfishing. They spearfish in the warm waters of the Bahamas. Their favorite fish to catch and eat is the hogfish!

CRABTREE Publishing Company

Written by: Kerri Mazzarella
Designed by: Kathy Walsh
Proofreader: Crystal Sikkens

Photographs: Shutterstock; Cover: ©Al McGlashan, ©MicroOne, ©Zerbor, ©GreyMoth; Pg 3, 4, 8, 12, 16, 20, 24 © ESB professional; Pg 1, 3, 6, 8, 16, 18, 20 © MicroOne; Pg 7, 10 ©Zerbor; Pg 4 ©YanLev; Pg 6 ©silvae; Pg 7 ©YanLev; Pg 8 ©David Carbo; Pg 9 ©Longjourneys; Pg 10 ©FtLaud; Pg 11 ©Al McGlashan; Pg 12 ©Zane Vergara; Pg 14 ©Fiona Ayerst, ©Martin Prochazkacz; Pg 16 ©Dudarev Mikhail; Pg 17 ©Drew McArthur, ©PixelSquid3d; Pg 18 ©Vitalii Nesterchuk; Pg 19 ©Sergio Sergo; Pg 20 ©FtLaud; Pg 21 ©metamorworks; Pg 22 ©Piotr Milewski; Pg 24 ©Amy Humphries on Unsplash; Pg 26 ©Rostislav Ageev; Pg 27 ©Madelein Wolfaardt; Pg 28 ©Allexxandar

Library and Archives Canada Cataloguing in Publication
CIP available at Library and Archives Canada

Library of Congress Cataloging-in-Publication Data
CIP available at Library of Congress

Crabtree Publishing Company
www.crabtreebooks.com 1-800-387-7650

Printed in the USA/072022/CG20220201

Published in the United States
Crabtree Publishing
347 Fifth Avenue, Suite 1402-145
New York, NY, 10016

Published in Canada
Crabtree Publishing
616 Welland Ave.
St. Catharines, Ontario L2M 5V6